Adv

Tally
the
Turtle
Tally Moves Away

tate publishing
CHILDREN'S DIVISION

April D. Dobson

Published by Tate Publishing & Enterprises, LLC
127 E. Trade Center Terrace | Mustang, Oklahoma 73064 USA
1.888.361.9473 | www.tatepublishing.com

Tate Publishing is committed to excellence in the publishing industry. The company reflects the philosophy established by the founders, based on Psalm 68:11,
"The Lord gave the word and great was the company of those who published it."

Book design copyright © 2013 by Tate Publishing, LLC. All rights reserved.
Cover and interior design by James Mensidor
Illustrations by Cleoward Sy

Published in the United States of America

ISBN: 978-1-62510-677-3
Juvenile Fiction / Animals / Turtlesry
13.02.14

"I am tired of living in the same place," said Tally Turtle.

"Me too!" said Fannie Fish.

"Well, I don't know about you," said Tally, "but I am going to move away."

"But where will you go? Where will you live?" asked Wilma Worm.

"I don't know, but Dover Pond has become really boring, so I am going to go somewhere else!" exclaimed Tally.

So Tally packed up his shell and said good-bye to Fannie Fish, Freddy Frog, Sammy Snake, Wilma, Woodrow, and Wanda Worm, and he was on his way.

"Whew!" exclaimed Tally. "It seems like I have been walking forever! I'll just go and take a little nap under the shade of that tree."

So Tally made his way to the tree, and just as Tally began to doze off, he heard a loud noise. *Vrr! Vrr! Vrr! Vrr! Vrr!* The noise grew louder and louder and began to make Tally a little scared.

"What's that noise?" exclaimed Tally. "Why it's...it's a lawn mower!"

Tally began running as fast as he could, and suddenly he was lifted by two little hands.

"Whoa! Put me down!" yelled Tally.

"Mother! Mother! Look what I found in the back yard!"

Why, I have been picked up by a little boy! thought Tally.

"Ooh! A turtle!" the little boy's mother exclaimed.
"Can I keep him, Mama? Can I?" the little boy cried.
"Well, I guess so, but you must find something to keep him in."

"Did you hear that? She said I can keep you! I am going to call you Mr. Tom," said the little boy. "Now you just stay right here on the floor, and I'll find a fish bowl for you to stay in."

"A fish bowl...? Why, I'm a turtle!" Tally exclaimed. "I have to get out of here!"

Tally ran as fast as he could, and before he knew it, he was back at Dover Pond with all his friends.

"Hi, everybody!" said Tally.
Tally was joyfully greeted by everyone as they all said hello and welcomed him back home.

"Hi, Tally! We thought you moved away," said Fannie Fish.

"Well, I did," replied Tally. "But I realized that the best place to be is here in Dover Pond with all my friends."

e|LIVE

---

listen|magine|view|experience

In your hands you hold a complete digital entertainment package. In addition to the paper version, you receive a free download of the audio version of this book. Simply use the code listed below when visiting our website. Once downloaded to your computer, you can listen to the book through your computer's speakers, burn it to an audio CD or save the file to your portable music device (such as Apple's popular iPod) and listen on the go!

How to get your free audio book digital download:

1. Visit www.tatepublishing.com and click on the e|LIVE logo on the home page.
2. Enter the following coupon code:
   54c3-0df7-4960-a9b1-9c73-28a9-08d4-0fbc
3. Download the audio book from your e|LIVE digital locker and begin enjoying your new digital entertainment package today!